THE
WOMB   IN   THE   HEART
&
OTHER   POEMS

The Womb In The Heart

&

Other Poems

Chimalum Nwankwo

African Heritage Press
San Francisco   Lagos
2002

AFRICAN HERITAGE PRESS

San Francisco
411 Randolph Street
San Francisco, CA 94132
USA
Tel: 415-469-8676
Fax: 415-661-7441
Email: afroheritage9760@aol.com
URL: www.africanheritagepress.com

Lagos
23 Unity Rd. Ikeja
Lagos, Nigeria.
Tel: 1-4972044

Library of Congress Control Number: 2001095831
    Nwankwo, Chimalum

Selections: 2002.
The Womb in the Heart/Chimalum Nwankwo
Poetry, African Studies, African American Studies, Multicultural Studies.

ISBN: 0-9628864-1-6.

DEDICATION
For
my mother
Janet Ulanwa Ike Nwankwo
Like the rest of us, no saint, but still...
my mother
&
more than a sacred avenue...

CONTENTS

Preface viii

PRYING...

Burst of Fires 2

The Revolution 4

A FLOWER...

Flower from the Tomb 9

UNDER THE SACRED UDALA TREE...

The Womb in the Heart 11

Lady Under The Mango Tree 17

A Chant for Charlatans 20

The Forbidden 27

Serene Images 32

Runners to Heaven 39

Ogbanje 47

August 29 51

Flower on the Way 53

And She Walked On 56

COOLING FIRES...

Libation at Noon 60

Colors of Loss 63

That Absence 65

Lost Compass 66

Waiting 68

Green Leaf 70

Breakers 71

Iroko in the Wind 72

The Return 73

Beach Sand in the Evening 75

Face in the Metro 76

A Reflection 78

She Stands Before Me 81

Flower of Morning 82

OF HISTORY...

The Spirits of Volubilis 85

& WAR...

Rodin in Biafra 88

TALES OF THEIR PASSING & POEMS FOR THE GENERAL...

Tales of Their Passing 91

A Song for the General's File 92

The Harmattan 93

A Song for their Second Coming 95

A Song for *Mgbedike* 97

OF SUCCESS...

A Chant of Success 101

Preface to *The Womb in the Heart*

This pretentious testament from an older poet will be found quite useless to fellow older poets whose systems and processes and mythologies have calcified with the bones of their art! It is bound to be of some sort of use to the young poet, (especially the younger African poet of like background) because of the tentativeness and exploratory gambits that have marked all careers, and blighted all private studies with the familiar mess of shreds and hidden scraps of the most dreadful or shameful of scribbles. Right now, I shake with guilt in the court of memory.

Poetry is a fiction of feelings, driven by spirits, guided by the benevolence of a mind in crisis and agitation of sorts. This strange and irrationally happy crisis triggers thoughts and feelings capable of re-agitating or pleasing readers, depending on emotional, psychological or spiritual kindred or constitution of the reader. That the other heart or mind responds is because the end of the poet coincides somewhat with that of the reader. It is therefore somewhat safe to suggest or assume that most poetry aims for various ends, mostly good. The reader could, of course, subvert the aim of the poet as many have subverted the sacred literature of many religions. In the light of that slightly dangerous probability, one thing the young poet must try to make a constant is avoidance of responses of perplexity. Unfortunately, most poets pass through that unhappy crucible before the purer flowers of their feelings begin to bloom. Again, I am guilty in the court of memory.

In general terms, the poet cannot afford to be neither understood nor felt. A poet must always offer something. If you are not understood, ah … not to worry. The criminal thing is not to be *felt*!!! It is from feeling that we find our way back to the labyrinth of meaning for clarification and hopefully, subsequent understanding.

A poetry reading audience or auditorium is a dangerous territory for all poets, young or old. People who congregate there cover a terrible spectrum in expectations. That spectrum stretches from a desire for twinkle twinkle little star to readiness for astral flights or at least some form of levitation. And all that, you know, cannot come from the goatskin bag or the laptop of one poet. The thing is to be as convincing as either a most virtuoso of actors or an empathetic drunk. Be ever ready to arrest your audience or reader with your own special unobtrusive verbal mind-cuff!!!

If your reader or listener utters that familiar lamentation : " I am sorry, but I did not understand a single phrase from all that stuff." Not to worry…Repartee? "But did you like it?" If the answer is yes, you have a partial success, and that is all you need. But if the answer is still in negative perplexity, you are in trouble! Two things are possible. You are dealing with either a dreadful earth-bound dummy or the brilliant modern fellow in a hurry tormented by bank accounts, taxes and investments, marriage and the uneven keel of human progress. The fellows probably only go to work, eat, drink and sleep. Flee from the former and be polite to the latter. Never be angry. But mark that your probable fan is the person who continues with. "...I like it, it is beautiful but I still do not understand it..." Find out why the fellow likes it. Reflect and work on the proffered reason/s for liking it, in your next poems...

Most real poets are usually foolish in their tolerant attitudes to their fellow human beings and the failings of humanity. Many are like inebriated lovers round the clock. Some, no matter how old, retain the virgin precocity of children. Some are nasty wits who mean no harm with their nastiness, but some times cause harm any way. You, of course, cannot resist forgiving them! Some times you run into poets whose conducts make you wonder whether they are not butchers or morticians. They have been lionized and acclaimed for writing very brilliant stuff which are bound to turn rancid and malodorous one year after their death. These are demonic frauds that you should stay away from because taint and contamination are quite easy. Believe me, I have never met a really brilliant or intelligent poet who is humane and spiritual or kind. You are probably baffled by all this. Be baffled because I know that there is something so sweet and tender about the real poets I have met. A different kind of brilliance and intelligence hide behind what strikes me more as humility for lack of a more sensitive and touching assessment or appreciation of their natures.

Distrust any poet who is brilliant and intelligent in the manner you associate with the erudite and calculating. Invariably, I have found the bully lurking behind the social facades of such personages. An older poet who still has the bully in his or her consciousness should be dreaded as a spiritually ineducable or incorrigible fraud. And believe me, that blight is very serious!

Distrust any poet who, without caveat, teaches or preaches to you about the rules and regulations of poetry . Such mentors want your creativity shackled. What you need is a certain kind of awareness that simply reminds you about what other practices and traditions have been. You can then generate your own system as part of the unstoppable process and order of enrichment that have become part of the growth of human arts and crafts in history. And for goodness sake, beware of the word *universal*. The con men of international politics have sacralized that word. They use it in various circumstances to un-self the unwary and inspirit them with their own national imps and demons. The imps and demons then transmute you forever into their obedient servants singing their anthems and war songs and dirges without behest like some surrealistic marionettes in the unstable dreams of the half drunk!

I have no doubts that you have heard gurus here and there warning you to stop writing poetry. Poetry, they say, is a *spent genre*. They will not tell you whose poetry. But you have also heard gurus of same ilk trumpeting about the *end of history*. They will not tell you whose history. Very soon, you will hear the same weird voices counseling you to stop eating pounded yam and *egusi* soup with your washed fingers, all in the name of the arrival of civilization. If you ask them about the significance of the packed and intense audiences in Nigeria when Chimalum

Nwankwo and some leading Nigerian poets give their readings, they will probably scratch their pretentious pates and try to mumble something intelligent. Do not worry. These gurus are merely trying to be *universal*, if you know what I mean.

Distrust any poetry founded on any ideology that has something to do with policing the human mind or foisting any codes on it. The human mind is a mystical criminal that can never be arrested! You can probably attempt a temporary detention. But that is as far as any one or system can push it. If you distrust this high flying counsel, simply go and verify from the living or dead leaders of the defunct Soviets. Or indeed ask some of their half dead and deaf clones and surrogates or expiring dictatorships in our capacious Africa.

All the tools for the making or construction of poetry and the poet are there in our tender years. They come to us through a double tutelage; the tutelage of the environment and the tutelage of our inner selves or world. Let me deal with the tools of the latter. The subconscious gathers them like tinders for future bonfires or conflagrations. Experience is their *ignis*. And that also gathers alongside the tinders. The poet's principal tool, words, slowly begin their aggregations, coalescing, and syllabic taxonomies at that time. It is a process which I see as the laying of the foundation stones for the sense of language. It is when we begin an internal education on potency. And potency has to do with elasticity in its finisphere. What I mean here is that realm where we are capable of discovering how far we can squeeze or stretch a word, to get out its last melisma in musicality and iota of meaning. I am so sorry to have to enforce the crazy old license of poetry here in this prose to explain what I mean…But essentially, what I am driving at is that an old man or woman cannot become a poet!!! He or she might be able to write good poetry but the bolstering lunacies of the calling will be absent. Without that holy lunacy, forget it! This claim is no doubt artistically or intellectually blasphemous and sacrilegious, and hopelessly arrogant. But arrogance is something that, of course, a poet cannot totally escape. That is because of the *priestly* thing that has always been associated with poets in all cultures. P.B.Shelley,the English Romantic did not help matters by claiming and insisting, you know, that poets are the unacknowledged legislators of the world. So forgive the poet who periodically becomes sententious. Our African dictators, God bless and damn their callous souls, usually catch such poets and lock them up for a while. So my friend, be careful with righteousness and its concomitant arrogance. Do not say nobody warned you!

I must stress that an old man or woman cannot become a poet because that will involve skipping the crucial tutelage of the creative monastery, where from the humility of learning how to deal with language, we acquire the other necessary humility which enables us to understand how to deal with our selves in relation to humanity. How else and when do we learn how to cure or exorcise or impair or control the power of that most horrible bully in all of us? And believe me, this bully is most active and virile when we are young. I am not a psychologist but I do not believe that this fact can be successfully impugned!

x

An old painter or writer of other genres could become a poet in later life, but an old school master or engineer cannot. Such fellows cannot understand the possession by spirits, the patience during such possessions, the required surrender, the final generative dare which drives expressions from the cumulus of gestations. It is this fact and allied circumstances which mark the young artist. Often the work of the young poet has devastating power, but that is all there is to it. In the chinks, you find a plenitude of indications of lack in control because of the critical lack in patience. So just as you find an obtrusive bully in the young poet, you will find another kind of bully in the old fellow who becomes a poet. You will probably find craft or message or some item or creative ingredient in saccharine or excessive proportion. I give some chance to the old painter or writer from other genres because such fellows have gone through like tutelage as the poet. They will probably come into the business with the residual lunacies from their own calling. And by the way, be extremely careful about my reckless use of the word "young" in this preface. It is a tricky and misleading word because a few souls out there land on this strange turf called Earth much older and wiser than you and I, one of God's very unfair arrangements. I find it as inexplicable and mischievous as awarding a sprinter a few secret meters before a race begins!!!

Haste is the chief enemy of the poet. Haste prevents the young poet from appreciating the tutelage of the environment. The young African poet has to appreciate this simple fact or write poetry without roots, or probably slip into the verbal somersaults that people mistake for poetry today. There is still a lot on which to base modern African poetry. The African environment is so rich in sounds and other technical facilities that the whole thing is astonishing. These sounds are there as ready resources from the indigenous languages, from the fermentations of syncretic processes and cultural diversity and their harmless craziness, or from the flora or fauna of the African world. The great American poet, Robert Frost, once said he was looking for an old-fashioned way to be new. In African poetry we can happily say that we have no old fashions, as long as we still accept the validity of the colonial languages as official languages in African countries. We should always be ready to *play* with those languages on our own terms while searching for our own distinctive voices. A poet without a distinctive voice is like the lumbering shadow of a nameless creature . And that is not what you want to be. Black musicians have demonstrated this fact all over the world. Listen carefully to black music from Latin America, the Caribbean, Cuba, the United States of America, and you will understand this point. Borrowing does not imply a lack of distinction, especially when borrowing is done most creatively, most functionally and most pragmatically. Borrow from anywhere, but do not forget your own identity. Your identity is like the hanger in your closet before you put the dress on it.

When I think of an arresting simplicity, I usually go to Chinese poetry. When I want the folksy, I go to Eastern Europe. When I want the romantic and hyperbolic, I go to the Middle East ; for the heavy brush of metaphors, I go to Neruda and the South Americans. *I stay with the traditional African (Igbo) base for the chief bolsters of my practice.* Since I am still writing in English, I visit the English metaphysicals, and Lord Tennyson for his captivating cymbals ; the American beat poets and Walt Whitman for symphonic simulations, especially to Langston Hughes, the great master of jazzy liesureliness. Forget this horrendous list! I am simply trying to suggest how far to rove while questing for identity and uniqueness of voice. Beware of what sticks out from roving. It could be quite an atrocity to behold. Like a live roach on a white shirt at a gala event!!!

Roving here and there for other tricks of the trade has not affected my everlasting mantra. Part of that mantra is that *I am an Igbo poet writing in English.* That apart, what I think about poetry is what universal theater practice says about a play. A play is not a play until it is staged. It is the stage-worthiness which makes it a play. In that same vein, a poem is not a poem until it has been read and heard, confirmed to possess both oral and aural intensity. The *good* word deployed effectively usually has both magic and penumbra! It resonates and evokes and makes the most innocuous extraordinary or forbidden. The good word is the holy usher in a good poem leading you gingerly from one portal of feeling to the other. The good word also doubles as an attendant to the secret switches of light in every atrium of meaning! The African base guarantees limitless resources for such results because of the callousness and innocence with which we domesticate all colonial languages. Serves our former masters right! The cursed Caliban thing!

See what our popular artists are doing with Western instruments for Congo music, the High life, even your Christian revivalists music. What those practitioners do with Western instruments could be done with the languages and the total African environment. I believe a similar point was made by Chinweizu and his friends regarding Jazz music in their famous book *Toward the Decolonization of African Literature.* I am beginning to sound almost intelligent. And that is not the purpose of this preface.

In this new volume, *The Womb in the Heart,* I have tried to demonstrate that it is possible for the African poet to do many things, very many different things. Drive your poetry like a car toward all possible pleasurable directions. But in your drive, understand that a driver who leaves his or her house cannot return there unless the routes of the drive and the mission or purpose of the drive are clear. Part of my mission in this new volume is to recognize in our African world the existence of what I call the deep dance, the dance of planets and of the revolution. The deep dance is a more concrete thing than the *aerial zone* which you may have encountered in one of my earlier volumes of poetry, *Toward the Aerial Zone.* The aerial zone is a mythical zone of *chalk* and brightness. It is a pure realm of goodness in human thought and action. I associate it with chalk because the Igbo regard chalk as a holy ritual symbol and marker of purity, like the *ogilisi,* the holy tree which the Igbo use for marking tombs and boundaries. There are of course other *open* poems, poems on more general and accessible *foundations.*

In the African collision with the Western world, so many things in African culture were damaged , and to some extent the African psyche. But even though many things remain damaged and irreversible, so many things picked up new steam in reconstructive accretion, shedding or weaving new identities from the damage. This condition of destruction and regeneration and endless flux appear to mark the character of the entire cosmos. We hear from the scientists something regarding the fearful heat of galactic expansion from endless regeneration of new bodies millions of light years in deep space. We cannot be insensitive to such wisdom in the name of cultural authenticity or independence. Africa is part of the Cosmic system. We cannot therefore operate in our art as if we live elsewhere.

The core of the poetry of *The Womb in the Heart* is an effort to come to terms with life and its unstable beauty in old and new loves, and poke at some facades of the perishable in a human environment full of the illusions of an end inside a world without end...

Chimalum Nwankwo
Lodge of the Spirit/Ndawi Ikuku Agbala
Ndikelionwu
Orumba County, Anambra State
NIGERIA

PRYING...

Burst of Fires

Now trembles my own galaxy
Heaving always with secret things

My life is now like deep deep space
It is now like the burst of great fires

It is like death shifting into life
Joining for ever the walk of snakes

It is now like the great rondure
The great circle of the aerial zone

The moon glow of the naked mothers
The white instant of the cross-roads

The sigh of relief at a puzzles end
The deep dance without the distances

The stars clear from all the ashes
And all ashes without milky ways

2

Like the old errors of the morning
The galaxy retreats in new explosions

It is a noontide of cooling fires
Unscorchable from knowledge of age

Like the new planets cooling away
Settling into orbits of the deep dance

Every spark now takes a clean name
With specks of ash blinding nothing

Drum beats come from all collisions
With new collisions in the new beats

The harmony writing love in space
Big crisis letters without fevers

Like age understood without pain

Or death read in petals of flowers

The great rondure reads the deep dance
In the inviolable walk of snakes...

3

My life tables now a clean testament
A dream recalled in the early morning

Where love is like a vase of fresh flowers
Flowers delivered from a master garden

Tombs and tombs mark the clean testament

Tombs pulsing hard for resurrections
Tombs pregnant with beats of the deeep dance

Tombs echoing the burst of great fires
Tombs reading all spaces like the womb

Where birth breaks the iron dome of death
And death becomes a flower in the tomb

And tomb and womb join the eternal walk
Where planets cool off like old loves

And the rondure repeats the coded dances
The walk of snakes in eternal cycles...

The Revolution

Okilikili bu ije agwo
           .... An Igbo saying
The walk of the snake is in cycles

1

The tomb will part its gates
Like the womb for all its bellows

Where suns and stars are forged
The foundry of the deep dance

But will follow the rising sun
The journey of fire to wells

Where mountains of old ashes
Become gold in moon glow

And silences loose their tongues
In the tumult of all cycles

From boulders to dust grain
The deep dance rules the drums

For the coded steps of mothers
Under the sacred udala tree

In the orbits of the planets
They read the spirit children

The prying eyes of their love
Their cries to see the world

Through the songs of naked mothers
Under the sweet udala tree

Divining the great fires
The tumbling glows in deep space ...

The tumbling of great fires
To the beats of the deep dance...

2

The snake reads the rondure
Follows the world in cycles

Reading the paths of planets
In the rhythm of the deep dance

Reading the paths to heaven
In the call of the naked mothers

Reading the spirit children
Their love for the deep dance

Reading peace in strikes
In the heart of final events

Reading the dance of mothers
Under the sacred udala tree

3

Combat plans in the making
But who reads the heart of morning

And combat plans in action
But who will pry deep nights

Who remembers the passage ways
The hammered pegs on cliff faces

In the great breeze of victory
Thundering into our hearts

In the memory of colonnades
In the journey under moon glow

The search for the naked mothers
Under the sweet udala tree

For lost in our first cries
Are memories of the deep dance

As our last cries forget
The coded dance of planets

The return to the colonnades
The forests to the seven rivers

And the love which frothed like wine
For the sacred udala tree

Between the great seven rivers
And the sacred udala tree...

4

Where is the pain in the heart
Where flowers mark the tombs

And the womb houses all
The bonfires and all their ashes

Where love comes in cycles
Where the snake learns the cues

That great everlasting walk
The walk of eternal cycles

The roots of the deep dance
The coded dance of mothers

Under the sacred udala tree
At the inviolable chalkways

The heart knows the heat
The fire of the splitting bud

And the heart knows the pain
The gold inside the forge

How creation dubs all cries
In desires of spirit children

And makes each pang a note
In the coded dance of mothers

Singing under the moon glow
Under the sacred udala tree..,

Love always falls like flakes
And settles into the womb

The great womb in the heart
From where sweet flowers bloom

Over all the tombs of death
And of pulsing resurrections

Like the tumblings in deep space
Echoes the spirit children

Where the great dance of planets
Beat rhythms for the deep dance

And echoes from the walk of snakes
Draw rhythms for the deep dance

And the spirit children come
In beat with the revolution

In beat with the great mothers
Naked under the moon glow

Waiting for the spirit children
Under the sacred udala tree

With their great prying eyes
Searching for the sweet fruits

Searching for the great mothers
Under the sacred udala tree

Where all the naked mothers
Will become sacred avenues

With their eternal beats
Under the sacred udala tree

Coded in the walk of snakes
And there in the deep dance

Under the sacred udala tree
Under the sacred udala tree...

A FLOWER...

Flower from the Tomb

Elegance of palms in gentle breeze
Grace of duikers on hind legs

Emulsion of twilight on calm beach water
Whose ripples must beat seven eyes

Water of the crescent moon
Bathing the jungle at sunset

O royal python toweled dry
Glistening too from lamplight of my soul

Always you made my lips quiver
Before a rainbow touched my heart

Between the morning and noontide of our meeting
I remained human with your incandescence

I was the rocket of all galaxies
Powered by bonfires of your heart

But this is evening ; evening of ashes
Endgame of skies breaking in invisible lines

Endgame of sand dunes of scorched lilies and roses
Of the short horizon of steel, marble cycloramas

Unless you sit on angel galleries
Blights will blaze over your serene image

You were alone on my royal seat
Matchless work by nameless genius

O sealed meaning of mysteries
Speeding through the white clouds of my night

You were what is left by a sacred tomb
A resurrection with a flower behind

You from the deep of the sweetest of dreams
Daring the dragon of sunlight...

UNDER THE SACRED UDALA TREE...

The Womb in the Heart

My mother told me that as teen-agers, periodically, they gathered naked in moonlight and sang and danced for many nights under the sacred udala tree. It was for the spirit children to see their beauty clearly, and choose who will be their mothers in the world. Husbands came soon after to pick them as brides. The nudeness was show for humans and spirits.

1

Of all beginnings
The womb is the head

The queens beauty glows
First from the diadem

The face may not know
Of the rivers in front

The womb is the head
The chair of kings

The throne of queens
The seed of the heart

In the womb of the heart
In the cache of memory

The womb is the tomb
For all beginnings

2

The moon glows
Over the udala tree

Burnish of new maidens
Waiting for children

Under the udala tree
At the gate of spirits

The moon glows
Waiting for children

For the nude maidens
Under the udala tree

3

The bellows are silent
Where the moon glowed

Over the gonads of gods
Under the udala tree

The red forge is cold
And the harmattan blows

Over ashes over eddies
Under the udala tree

The great flames are dead
The tongues are no more

The tongue which licked the sky
Under the udala tree

4

The queen has left the king
And the ring of fires

From the mountains of festivities
And the bonfires of passions

The halls of ears are vacant
From cavorts and revels

Under the udala tree

Where the throats of gold humbled
The school of finest birds

And daylight wore a forever face
Blossoms are now stories

Over the udala tree

Who dances for kings now

Under the udala tree

5

And then I found the words
Mole of festive chambers

I, dumb participant
Child spirit of the formal universe

Enemy of diamond fires
Mantled by the spirits

I found all the tombed words
Under the udala tree

After the nude maidens
After the coded dances

After the festivities
And my robe of rags

After the children had come
After the children had gone

And the nude maidens
Had become sacred avenues

And my words their elements
Ushers of ghosts to gods

Witnesses of transformations
Ushers of ghosts and gods

Far from the udala tree...

6

So who shall hear me now
Far from the udala tree

The red forge is cold
Under the udala tree

The bellows are quiet
Under the udala tree

And the nude maidens there
Now are sacred avenues

7

These words are the votives
For the lost celebrants

Treasures from pregnancies
Chosen things from spirits

Images from the resurrects
Under the udala tree

Puzzling images from spirits
Under the udala tree

8

From those silent bellows
The stoppered silences

Thunders in retreat
Into wispy stories

Into weightless clouds
In the womb of the heart

And the bellows are quiet
From the wispy stories

Heavy rains there in retreat...
Under the udala tree

9

The womb of the heart
Is the haunt of hearts

Echo station of all journeys
And gold cup of exhalations

When the public square shakes
From the thunder and tumult

From the tumult and thunder
Of departures and returns

The womb distends and is astir
The tomb of many births and deaths

Of exquisite flowers
And of grotesque plants

Of surprising resurrections
And of strange perditions

Salvation is uncertain
Under the udala tree

Echo station of all journeys
And gold cup of exhalations...

10

When the red forge is quiet
Under the udala tree

And the nude maidens
Have become sacred avenues

And the spirit children
Have chosen all their mothers

And all the great races
Have been won and lost

And the glow of the moon
Has nothing for our hearts

And we turn our faces
From all faces wizened

And ginger Time descends
In its judges parachute

Salvation is uncertain
Under the udala tree

For ashes are supreme
Under the udala tree

Echo station of all journeys...
Echo station of all journeys...

Lady Under The Mango Tree

At Ezinkwo village in Ndikelionwu, there is a lady in a shop under a mango tree where the sacred udala tree used to stand...

1
Lady under the mango tree
Do you know where you are

Lady under the mango tree
Under shower of neon

Lady under the mango tree
The moon shines over you

Under shower of neon
The moon shines over you

2
Lady under the mango tree
Do you feel the moon glow

Do you feel the power of neon
And light without the planets

The power of the deep dances
Ordering the revolution

Do you feel the walk of snakes
The chill of the labyrinths

The breeze of the colonnades
Between all the buried dances

Between all the seven rivers
And the mango tree in moon glow

The touch of flaming songs
Of old ash and dust airborne

Of burnt desires for secret things
Of the earth ready to explode

Of moon wash and holy tingles
Branding you with the revolution

The deep dance of planets
Coded in the dance of mothers

The wan face of the moon
Smiling at the neon lights

With the suns fire kisses
Smiling at the neon lights

Lady under the mango tree
What do you feel today

3

There is a rampage in the air
A stampede of iron hoofs

Neon and the moon at war
But the lights are still shining

Lady under the mango tree
Two lights are now shining

Here under this mango tree
Do you feel the revolution

The pain of the shriveled navel
The braid of life and death

The nectar of the burdened dialogue
Of the heavy and great envelope

Mute echoes of sweet explosions
Of deep and secret things

Mysteries jostling for resurrections
Of new tapers and of new banners

With you as the great mother
With new steps for the deep dance

The dance of all the planets
Dance of the revolution

Hanging there in moon glow
Covered in shower of neon...

4

My palm is an empty treasury
Full of lines of the deep dance

Lady under the mango tree
I offer my palm to you

With shadows of the colonnade
And of the great passageways

Leading the spirit children
Toward the lilting notes

With nights invisible garlands
Gracing the great mothers

I accept the gift of night
Moon glow over neon shower

The thing behind secret doors
The gold in yesterdays pain

I will count my wares in neon
I count them too in moon glow

I will read their silks of promises
And measure them in the steps

In the dance of the revolution
In the coded dance of mothers

Under the sacred udala tree
There in the womb of the heart

Where flowers wait in tombs
For resurrections and new deaths...

A Chant for Charlatans

For Obioma Nnaemeka, Ifi Amadiume and all those African women laboring to draw lines between the charlatans and the naked mothers who danced in moon glow under the sacred udala tree ...

I

Today, my mother
Is the day of charlatans

They do not know the way
 Or the gate of spirits

They did not show their bodies
 To the spirit children

And they did not bathe

Under the moon glow

And so they do not know
The first step of the deep dance

2

T'he rhythms of their cry
 Blaze fires through the rafters

And the throats of vultures
And the throats of hawks

Remain the well spring
Of their chants of sorrow

Pastors of dusk at dawn
Sharing with the crow

Bands of white at noontide
The owls mystic eyes in the day

But the hyenas are laughing
 At their sorrows in the night

For hyenas sense a carcass
Of souls laughter signals

The signals of frustrations
Signals of coming dinners

For no sun ever shines
From the middle of a storm

From behind stony barricades ...
Nor from the stony barricades ...

3

And at the sight of blazons
Glaring at the serene village

The callused women rise
Like ghosts from their graves

Their tired breasts are bare
Their feet have tasted fires

With voices hoarse with pain
The planets rock with cries

Charlatans   Charlatans —

Do the charlatans hear those wails
The pain from genuine hearts

Can testaments in stone
Ever come from human hearts

Charlatans   Charlatans —

Who comes in alien blazes
Far from the udala tree

From where the spirit children
Chose their great mothers

With their nakedness moon-washed
Ogilisi fencing their souls

With great bodies in spirit fires
Under the sweet udala tree

Bodies of blazing light
Gold polished from moon glow..

4

But who come in alien blazes
Nude in decks of finery

Charlatans   Charlatans –
Is the roar of restive crowds

They see through the rouge
And through the mascara

Charlatans   Charlatans –
Is the roar of restive crowds

And through those great tears
From the crocodiles haunts

Charlatans   Charlatans –
Is the roar of restive crowds

Faces of buried blushes
Red worries from frigid zones

Charlatans   Charlatans –
Is the roar of restive crowds

For the white rings of wizards
Around the seven eyes

Charlatans   Charlatans
Is the roar of restive crowds

White on brows for beauty
Burials of great visions

Charlatans   Charlatans –
Is the roar of restive crowds

Daylights for the black goats

No use in wings of night

Charlatans   Charlatans
Is the roar of restive crowds

Their visions are refracted
Not for the souls agonies

But the bleating of their hearts
For that sweetness of power

Charlatans   Charlatans
Is the roar of restive crowds

Tapers of thin delight
 Flares in blizzards of time

Charlatans   Charlatans –
Is the roar of restive crowds

Note of a crescent moon
Night of steel in envelope

Charlatans   Charlatans
Is the roar of restive crowds

Silk threads for hidden feelings
Steel hoofs for other hearts

Charlatans   Charlatans
Is the roar of restive crowds

5

O Mandala
Gift of the orient stage

Do those who dance for power
Not dance in a circle

To arrow their hearts
Into the bulls eye of love

To draw from the souls wells
Diamond testaments

23

Rain-makers have forgotten
The ladders to the clouds

The secrets of the rain stone
Buried in fonts of fairness

A flowers beauty explodes
With zero sound or storm

Their gunpowder is lit
From deep roots in the earth

But charlatans wish to float
And forget their dew earth

But what great mage forgets
The farm of all the cowries

The cornerstone of great walls
Which houses womb and tomb

The fountain of all blood
The base rock of gyrations

For the dances of the heart
Love begins with flowers

For flowers are the ballasts
For the seeds of all hearts

The mast of hearts in flight
The potion of morrows

Love comes in twin laughters
Dew from the sky of souls

But to floods of restive crowds
What do the charlatans cry :

Believe me my people
Love comes in grenades

Believe 0 my people
Love comes in grenades

But how can love bear grenades
Grenades in rains of blood

When the Earth Goddess and the spirits
Forbid blood on all their turfs

What keeper of fine treasures
Will love a feast of skulls

Will mount pennants and buntings
For rogues with eyes of fire

Will flag and drive the hot winds
Toward the seven rivers

Toward the spirit gates
Through the great colonnades

Of ushers of ghosts and gods
Watched by ogilisi trees

The sentinels forever
At the great spirit gates

6

Charlatans in the valley
Will not dream of mountains

From where the great hearts
Espy the sacred avenues

Between the nude mothers
And the spirit children

Between the red forge
And the holy great halls

Where in robes of flames
The ancestors brand the palms

For the urn of the naked mothers
The staff of serene images

For the stalwarts heart of rock

25

And the reedy voice of cowards

To mark the great deep sheets
With lines of the deep dance

The great dance of planets
Coded in the naked mothers

Their dance under moon glow
Under the sacred udala tree ...

7

In the vatic forest of worlds
Each shadow knows its light

Each snail carries its house
Each millipede reads its paths

Each blind bird knows its tree
As each poet finds a timbre

Knowing that planets without light
Must live by the grim rule

The rogues who rule the barns
Will pick the fattest yams

Will serve who wins their smiles
Like the rogues with longest knives

When the gunman has no bullets
Before the longest knives

They read the revolution
The dance of all the planets

They read the angry cries
The roars of restive crowds

Wailing for great mothers
Pain flowing in smolders.

Charlatans Charlatans !!!

The Forbidden

For the young African woman who does not know what my mother told me. This knowledgable young woman told me that she is the forbidden fruit . She is only able to love women. She will neither marry, have children, nor ever have anything to do with men. Intimacy with men is always a violent and oppressive thing. In that case, I assured her that what we all call God must be a reckless, wicked ,and irrational force. I remain quite certain that she will never understand that deep dance of naked mothers under the sacred udala tree...

1

Light falls from the moon
Under the sweet udala tree

From heavens cave of gold
Rain for the udala tree

Light and rain for the spirit children
Under the sacred udala tree

Light for the naked mothers
Rain from the spirit gateways

Light and rain under moon glow
Under the sacred udala tree

2

The moon shows its pregnancies
Gleaming gold in its smile

A smile of borrowed gold
For the sacred udala tree

With memories of naked mothers
Under light of revolution

The light of the great changes
Of passage ways everlasting...

3

Air returns to us as rains
In the secret silences of holy gifts

27

And so the spirits return always
To the sacred udala tree

To read the dust of sacrifice
Under the sweet udala tree

Where the coded dance of mothers
Shakes the great spyglass

Feeling for the wrapped cries
At all the gates of the womb

Answering to the great forge
Lessons from the planets dance

Answering to the great ways
In the light of the revolution

The power in the bole of things
In the light of the revolution

As air returns in rains
With the fanfare of mothers

With drums over the earths roof
With drums for the new dancers

And for the host of spirit children
Dancing for our great mothers

Under the sweet udala tree
Dancing for our great mothers...

4

Between that here and hereafter
Wrapped in one womb and tomb

The dance steps have been blocked
And the dance steps chalked in white

Who laughs at our naked mothers
Laughs before the great mirror

28

Who jibes at the spirit children
Claws at the cords of their coming

And laughs at our comings and goings
And at the inviolable   chalkways

Who sneers at the revolution
Laughs before their gaping graves

Laughs at the great boulders
Dancing in the great spaces

From where the great wine keeper
Chuckles at our festal fevers

In this ungated yard of iron dreams
Where rust is the soul of all moments

Where all the tenants are known
Like the golden secret of clowns

Where supplicants quest for rooms
At the knobs of crumbling doors

Where the boats of all our agonies
Match all the crimes in our hearts

In this short-circuit of all our laments
In front of the great iroko doors

Where all the seven rivers gather
In the great horizons pocket...

At the terminus of all our pants
And the drain of all our woes

In the great horizons pocket ...
In the great horizons pocket...

5

I have read the notes of planets
Surrendered to their secret dance

29

I have read the green vegetation
Surrendered to their secret dance

I have read the butchers knives
Surrendered to their secret dance

I have read the graveyards shovels
Surrendered to their secret dance

I have read the speech of flowers
Surrendered to their secret dance

I have read the seeds of yams
Surrendered to their secret dance

I have read the storms of oceans
Surrendered to their secret dance

I have read the depths of nights
Surrendered to their secret dance

The great epic of the desert sand
I have not read it in tears

The tornadoes red epitaphs
I have not read it in tears

The hurricanes roars of ghouls
I have not read them in tears

6

My heart sees seasons of tumult
But its heaven of dew is constant

So its thousand fires over secret fires
Is the crackling of diamond works

And my life blossoms in its glows
And draws from their nuggets of light

And I remember the fullness of first yams
Their whiteness and fibers of sweetness

And I remember the songs of harvest
And when time will shrivel all tubers

And I know why our mothers danced
And why the spirit children came

And why the moon glow was golden
Under the sacred udala tree

And why the moon was chosen
To light the great passage ways

7

So why forbid the great dances
For the light of the revolution

And who without God-cause
Forbids the light of the revolution

Forbid the light of eternal motions
Of elements in warm gyrations

Forbid the dance of naked mothers
The prying eyes of the spirits

And the dance of all the planets
Under the sacred udala tree...

Serene Images

*My mother told me that the aged were **okenye(okoha)**, serene images, sacred fruits of time. They were afraid of nothing, not even Death. They lived a simple life, revered by all. They were known for their courage in crisis circumstances, and would tell the blunt truths even at the risk of their lives. The welfare of the community remained uppermost in their lives. They fell to no manner of temptation, material or human. To tell the truth at that age was a service to humanity, the spirits, and Chukwu, the great God.*

Sacred fruits of time
& Serene images

Keepers of sacred avenues
The venerable ones

Where shall we find them now
I have seen the second coming

Of monsters from goldstone
Driven by diamond hearts

I have seen the second coming
Of night masks at noon tide

I have seen the second coming
Of the demon wedding

Of the apocalypse of hearts
At the out-dooring of the still-born...

Sacred fruits of time
& Serene images

2

The grand procession then
Bypassed the udala tree

Aware of the naked mothers
Of the great beats of their deep dance

Aware of eyes of the spirit children
The role of blood at the sacred avenues

Aware of the light of the moon
And the forge of the bellows

Aware of the sweetness of fruits
Bitter leaf for them in the morning

Aware of the prying eyes
Of the spirit children

Aware of the secret heavings
At the gate of spirits

Aware of the great traffic
In the colonnades and passage ways

Between the seven rivers
And the sacred udala tree

Their seven eyes trained for harvest
Divining the horizons of drums...

3

Sacred fruits of time
& Serene images

They will not touch the old wine
Forsaken by two markets

They will not touch that palm wine
Meant for the head hunters

For the great revolution
The night thing offers blessings

For that water and the light
From the deep wells of blood

For the fields where women
Dream of the naked mothers

Of the lucky hands of spirit children
And of the sacred avenues

And of the sweet udala tree...

The human niche in the revolution...

4

Sacred fruits of time
& Serene images

Serene images come from far away
From the earth over buried glass

In pieces with pieces of shattered pots
The great foundry of wisdom

When glass becomes for other faces
And new pots for the health of others

When appetites wait in suspension
In pension of spirits for other souls

For new witnesses for new births
Bearing news of the revolution

From the dance of naked mothers
And moon light over the udala tree

Bearing news of the revolution
Wisdom from the dance of planets

5

Serene images
& Sacred fruits of time

What teeth will grind
The final refuge of the great light

From the moon glow and everlasting hall
And from the sacred avenues

After the sight of variegated deaths
What heart wedded to the iroko

With sinews from the forge of planets
And the moon glow under the udala tree...

Tremors at the sound of knocks
Cold ruffles from the great curtains

What wind shakes the crease of wisdom
Pulsing with throbs of the deep dance

Heart bonded to the root of trees
In colonnades in the sacred avenues

Twin heart of the naked mothers
Beating in rhythm with the deep dance

The secret dance of planets
The dance of the revolution

6

Sacred fruits of time
& Serene images

Night stirs with sacrificial dreams
And daytime shakes with crashing trees

Of asphalt odors sweat-driven
Rolling over thorns and teeth of stone

Great vistas broken by the oracle
From the deep groves of the mind

White chalk guides their path
Like torrents of the first rains

Desert and sea listen to their claims
For the mind is the great oracle

Where the white chalk picks the cues
For the foothold on the marble cliffs

7

Sacred fruits of time
& Serene images

Their anklets are white threads
The deep colors of the aerial zone

They will not refract the suns kisses
Or bear gold from robbers dreams

Their cloths sit on their shoulders
The dignity is not empty

The weight is from poor folks
Heavy memories of poverty

Their chests are bare at noon
Their hearts are open parcels

They do not have like bats
Any reasons for their flights at night

They love the corn cobs message
When the sun confirms their message

And so with royal umbrellas
Truth is the serf of their breaths

These sacred fruits of time
Witnesses of the great revolution

Twin heart of the naked mothers
Witnesses of the deep dance

These sacred fruits of time
And these serene images...

8

This day is the day of sad vomits
Carrion from carnivores spews

Day of the drenched images
Reeking with the blood of mendicants

Day of the sacred fruits
Hanging from the tree of putrescence

Day of the hobbling quarries
Lost in the jungle of mad dogs

Day of the cannibal feast
Of body paint in brushes of blood

Listen to the skies of their hearts
Ruffling with banners of fear

Truth comes in the whisper of ants
And their planets heave in terror

Poverty holds the flagpole
It is a march of skeletons

Great ogres are serene images
They take the bows of skeletons

Death yells into the deep dance
Blighting the sacred avenues

With terror raging in the colonnades
And clouds over the moon glow

And demon armies of darkness
Ruling the udala tree

To halt the deep dances
The dance of the revolution

9

Sacred fruits of time
& Serene images

What happens to the naked mothers
The dance under the moon glow

What happens to the revolution
The secrets of the deep dance

The dreams of the naked mothers
Whispered by the trees

What happens to the spirit children
Their desire for the udala fruit

What will the moon wash
Under the sacred udala tree?

Runners to Heaven (with oja flute and drums in anti-phonal)

*They ask me always how I will spend eternity. I smile and talk about our hearts,
the jostling and the games in the womb in the heart, about the robbers already in
heaven. I respond as curiously as their hearts...*

1

The runners to heaven
Bypass the udala tree

Bypass the moon glow
And clutch at neon lights

Far from the moon glow
Beyond the udala tree

Beyond the deep dances
Under the udala tree

2

The runners to heaven
Bypass the great mothers

And the spirit children
Under the udala tree

3

They miss the colonnades
The navel of the planets

Between all the rivers
And the sweet udala tree

4

The runners to heaven
Bypass the gate keepers

The hammering and thunder
The heaving of the boulders

5

They miss the deep dance
Rumbling there in space

The galaxy and eddies
Coded by the mothers

6

They miss the great steps
The heating and the cooling

The dance of revolutions
Under the udala tree...

7

The runners to heaven
Bypass the sweet fruits

They want the avenues
From robbers stilettos

8

The blood of innocents
Is the tonic of their wiles

And their markets are empty
With heavy grim shadows

9

And scarlet threnodies
Barb their sleepy air

And the great womb shakes
With aborted dreams

10

And beads of stifled beats
Tomb in peoples sweats

Coded by the mothers
In haven of moon glow

11

And the spirit children pry
Under the udala tree

Unseen by the runners
Under the udala tree

12

These runners to heaven
Those runners to heaven

They do not see the robbers
Singing there in heaven

13

Robbers sing in heaven
Far from the udala tree

And the runners are wild
Far from the udala tree

14

Dust cakes over the cross
Standing in calvary

And robbers sing in heaven
Far from the moon glow

15

Runners to heaven wail
With robbers there in heaven

And a bloody rain falls
For a child in Bethlehem

16

And time spreads hoods
In the womb in the heart

With policed resurrections
Of runners and robbers

17

Their mountain roads are low
Like valleys and plains

Because of all the riots
In their hearts and heads

18

With ignorance at war
With the dubious demons

They swear from a book
Which time has laced with rust

19

There is rust in chapters
With absences howling

For all the spirit children
Of the great colonnades

20

No angel knows in heaven
No demon knows in hell

Why all the holy lands
Are wet with rains of blood

21

Why hatred wears a crown
The driver of their dreams

And robbers sing in heaven
Before the chant of runners

22

These runners to heaven
Bypass the golgotha

And the gardens of agony
And the cross at calvary

23

Runners sing of sacrifice
They dream of bloody springs

Like thunder in the evening
Faking rain in promises

24

Who mocks the spirit children
And the empty passageways

Who mocks the naked mothers
But do not know their dance

25

Who makes a rain of songs
Without sacrificial rams

With fountains in their hearts
With phantom trees in dreams

26

The runners to heaven
Grow flowers in their heads

Great flowers in their heads
With no blooms in moon glow

27

Hot winds command a hush
In the desert of their cries

And runners to heaven sing
And pulse like drums of war

28

The runners to heaven
Go dancing with robbers

Far from the udala tree
Go dancing with robbers

29

The passageways are barred
With steel from angry gods

Far from all the colonnades
Far from the moon glow

30

The naked mothers danced
The dance of all the planets

The dance of revolutions
Under the udala tree

31

These runners to heaven
Bypass the moon glow

With hunger in their steps
In their desert passageways

32

There is fear in their hearts
In the wells of their minds

Their colonnades stand in space
With no anchors for their roots

33

The runners to heaven
Miss the beats of the dance

The dance of naked mothers
Under the sacred udala tree

34

A world of owls and crows
With wild hyenas laughing

Fill their runners hearts
With songs of sterile trees

35

I hear their songs of love
I see what beats my mouth

I see their rainbows bole
Where angels hiss for adders

36

Their moon is glowing red
Their tree of love is cursed

Their road to heaven is dirt
Far from the udala tree

37

Their sun is hot and blind
With no kisses for the moon

No memories of the rivers
No singing and no dancing

38

No spirit children prying
At the beauty of the mothers

Coding the dance of planets
Under the udala tree...

39

The runners to heaven
Bypass the moon glow

Arrive there in heaven
Dancing with the robbers

40

Far from the moon glow
Far from the deep dance

Dance of naked mothers
Under the sweet udala tree...

Ogbanje

1

Perhaps you decided well
To choose the colonnade

To stroll between the great rivers
And the sweet udala tree

For the sweetness of the bean
And the sweetness of the pod

The pathway everlasting
To live there in moon glow

To watch and gloat forever
Over the dance of naked mothers

The dance of all the planets
Under the sweet udala tree

2

Perhaps you decided well
To stay there in moon glow

And be there in the heart
And the comfort of the womb

Not know the dome of death
And the darkness without selves

To keep the prying eyes
On the beauty of the dance

On the everlasting fires
From the breath of galaxies

And pulse with silent things
Blushing there in moon glow

At the beauty of the mothers
Under the sweet udala tree

3

Perhaps you decided well
To stay there in moon glow

With the rondure for a home
No dot between one line

But the line everlasting
Like the eternal walk of snakes

Led by all the chalkways
From the seven eyes at once

To be the soul of distance
In all the distances

To be there in the dance
In the eyes of all the codes

And live beyond the pain
Of the sacred avenues

Bred under moon glow
Under the sacred udala tree

4

Perhaps you decided well
To stay there in moon glow

The everlasting trophy
Which no dance can claim

Beyond the smile of queens
Beyond the fist of kings

The veneer of the flesh
Of the great serenity

Which houses well the soul
In the womb in the heart

Where the dance of naked mothers
The galaxy and the drums

Read and block the cues
Of the eternal walk of snakes

Under the great moon glow
Under the sweet udala tree

5

Perhaps you decided well
To stay there in moon glow

The joy between the seasons
The unscored and treasured beat

The void before the fires
Before the brand of naming

The great unchartable moment
Before the flash of birth

In the safety of the innocence
Before the awe of difference

How lovely then to know
The holy barren air

Wrapped in the song and dance
In the beauty of the mothers

In the fire of the deep dance
Before the prying eyes

In the saunter under the moon
Under the sweet udala tree

6

Perhaps you decided well
To stay there in moon glow

There must be joy there
As the jewel of permanence

There must be fullness too

49

In the link between the chains

Of what lives inside the deep
In the sea of human thought

For what shades the colonnade
Toward the udala tree

For what rules the balance
In the tension of wires

For what rolls the love songs
From the lips of mothers

Dancing there in moon glow
Under the sweet udala tree

7

Perhaps you decided well
To rule the great colonnades

Between the great rivers
And the sacred udala tree

Forever be in the dance
The deep dance of planets

In the coded dance of mothers
Dancing there in moon glow

Under the sacred udala tree...

August 29 (for Ogu)

Poem of the after-birth
Of the surf receding

Pearl of the panting breath
Of the great dialogue

Between beach sand wetness
And the roar of spent waves

Echo of music of the trees
In the colonnade to the mothers

Sheen of the sacred images
Burnished under glow of the moon

What do we have today
In our noon of pale rainbows

2

Poem of the after-birth
Brooch for the secret nuptial

Who will not pluck a flower
Blooming there by the way

Who will not dream of the silences
Between the breaker and wetness

Between the moment of light
And the imponderable gloom

Between the suspended vow
And the final bells of joy

The travelers dream in the rain
Wails for the knob of home

3

Poem of the after-birth
With the power of the day of birth

The lateness of the nuptials
Is buried in the festal mirth

No blemish there in a beauty
When a heart holds up the lamp

And wool is a thousand crags
Where tomorrow keeps the furrows

Like crowns of the mountain top
In the mountain climbers dream

With garlands and garlands
Which only the heart can see...

Flower on the Way (for the cheek)

1

That flower on my way
That I did not touch

It played with my heart
And I did not touch

A sweet game began
When my body was touched

By that flower on the way
Which I did not touch

My body and my heart
In an art everlasting...

2

No one will win
When a flower on the way

In that art everlasting
Ropes the combat ring

With bells from the moon
Commanding the body

Like the naked mothers
Commanding the children

With beauty and magic
Under the udala tree

Ruling with the moon glow
Under the udala tree

That flower on the way
Commanded the body

Playing with the heart
Like the mothers in moon glow

What body will not fail
In the art everlasting

When hearts dance to drums
In echoes of nude mothers

3

Up in the morning sun
That flower rose with me

And it played with me
That flower on the way

And it played with me
There till evening

And we went into the gold
Of the sunsets tarmac

That flower on the way
Just played with me

And I plucked the flower
With pain in my heart

For I knew in fear
That the flower on the way

Is a flower in the mind
Which will rule with the mind

4

And the sky was touched
With bonfires of stars

Like a prayer answered
In a night of storms

And a red horizon glowed
In a dream of rains

Of thunder and blue lightning
With lulls uncertain

But peace in green sheen
Projects draping fields

And the body and the heart
Like murmuring waves

Worship the surrender
In a sweet submission

Of folks in the country
Before a virgin moon

A prayer from the heart
For this flower on the way

Which blessed the war
Between body and heart

In this game of spirits
In an art everlasting...

And She Walked On (Contemplating her in the twilight)

At the portals she did not pause
And the rivers did not daunt her
And the wilderness was a home
Whatever the denizens offered
Her goals were in her palms
Lit by brands at the passage ways

And she walked on—

The cries of birth and life
Thunders and evening breezes
She was in the lullaby
As she was in all the dirges
All the notes were one
Key wind in the heart of a storm

And she walked on —

The jewel of the nude mothers
Under the sacred udala tree
The gold in the moon glow
The gong in the piths of their songs
Favored fruit of the night
When the spirit children came

And she walked on—

Her back was not the mat
Not the dream of noble chiefs
Not the stalwarts whistling call
She read the favored heart
Not in the rumbling of the blood
But in wheels spun by her mind

And she walked on—

The children picked the fruits
They picked her beauty too
Each read their kindred early
And marched toward the deep dance
Chalking bold the colonnades
And faint memories of *ogilisi*

And she walked on—

Daughter of royalty
Royalty in the head
And royalty in her soul
Not the glitter of a crown
Not the sheen of her beads
Not the leadership of maidens
Could dull all her gaits

And she walked on—

Into the thunder of marriage
And the agony of the big house
The cries were one to her
Of the children who chose her
And of those she found
Under the sweet udala tree
Or the passageways of stone

And she walked on—

And she would have survived
If husbands came from steel
From a cannon burst of bubbles
If firewood for life is stone
And village streams were geysers
And the rain winds blew
From the heart of demon fires

And she walked on—

She held her shoulders up
When the sky fell on her
As she held up her head
At clamors from the shadows
From the sun and stars of her heart
Blazing at the distances
Rolled into the deep dance

And she walked on—

She was secure always
Like all trees with deep roots
And she wrote her destiny too

The way her *chi* wrote it
With the lamps from her head
Her tendons hammering thoughts
Into time for women's fortunes

And she walked on—

To the glory of those children
Whose eyes had marked her beauty
Under that glow of the moon
And the glory of the one
Who saw her body first
Wrapped in the deep dances
Under the sweet udala tree

And she walked on—

Proud of the coded beats
Of the dance in moon glow
Of who read all the dances
Beating for all the flowers
Buried there in the womb
In all the tombs in the heart
The seat of resurrections

And she walked on—

Toward the seven rivers
Through the great colonnades
Fenced by *ogilisi* trees
With the passageways pulsing
With the music of her return
With storms in quiet eddies
Swirling round her cenotaph...

And she walked on—

COOLING FIRES...

Libation at Noon (for orc)

I pour this wine onto this earth
To who grants all secret powers

Pull the strings again and touch my heart
I need nothing and no one else
To scale the ramparts of my dreams

Where else is peace today
A digital rain falls all over the globe
And all vegetation is iron and plastic
The harvesters arrive always in time
The band of their coming blares in crisp notes
Their power of seduction is sweetest wine
The fruits of a synthetic vine of grapes
Or of palm trees under bastard care
Who will not bow has not been born

Great hordes clack all over this globe
Their diamond flag poles hoist banners for gold
From horizon to horizon nothing is different
And millions are in choirs for a lone God
From the great cacophony of their phony chants
Wild bandits find their fuels for blood
But who is bandit and who saint
When bandit and saint burn one candle

My brothers are falling in love with each other
And my sisters bury each other with kisses
Fear mounts sentry at the gates of their hearts
When every human breath is a tornado
Beyond our demon passions and fires
What can the warm dew offer a desert
Whose eyes will open in a great wilderness
Quaking in fear of digital rains

I have learned to look into your eyes
For the key and ladder to the ramparts
I know the pagan earth of that universe
I can find sleep there on the bare floor
And end my one-eyed vigil for my head
Where else can one find peace today

I have learned to listen to your laughter
The heart takes from it the great drumsticks
With which you beat my hearts marching song
A song of birds in my village morning
Known by blushing rainbows in twilight
From the birds notes of rippling waves
I learned how to ride the calm calm waters
From its empty beach to its countless shores

And in all contours of your pagan home
I have learned where to go and not to go
What the gongs say for alarum
And what they say for the holy ascent
When the clouds begin to gather us in their wings
And when the thunder of blood explodes over us
For that rebirth from the flames of flowers

2

This cry is like a testament in white noon
When humans and spirits hold their breaths
At the atrium of a thousand passage ways

For you I have crossed the great boundaries
Frightful to some like the seven rivers
I have given all for the ramparts of my dreams
I have made you the tape of a great race
And I must breast it again and again
For the astral glory of the pounding heart

I hear the roar from the vine of flowers
Over the holy cave for trysting hearts
With glowing petals on trembling trellises
I see spirals of incense around your image
Quivering to arias of softest music
There in the shrine of the mother of stars

I will forever return for worship
Where else can one find peace today
I am drunk in the safety of the elastic moments
In that pagan world of clouds with stairs
Where each rung is an endless field
Fields of the finest horses from our thoughts
Reined only by the panting of our hearts

Send down the ladder again for the ramparts
I will follow into the wells of your eyes again
And up to those mountains of the simple dreams
Dreams of our horses in open spaces
And go where the gales of your laughter drive us
Beyond the sounds of the trumpets of gold
Far from the shadows of the new vegetation
Choking the globe from digital rains.

Colors of Loss (for ET)

I will leave my giant door open
It is carved from hardiest iroko
The vagrant wind like callous love bangs it at will
It has banged the door a thousand times on the lintel
The cement and caulk are full of fissures
I will not touch the dust and fallen pieces
And I will neither clean nor repair any thing
Let the wind swing my door again
Each swing is a wicked blow in my heart
Not just because of the sweetness of the past
But because of the memory of how you closed it —
You closed it as if you did not mean it

It has been such a long long time
And now I know you may never come back
But I will leave my iroko door the way you left it
My walls will grow like prison walls grow
Mystic steel in the mind of one who knows it is the end
Only the hangman has the forbidden keys
The walls fall only in the morning of death

So I will touch nothing, my love
The wine glass, half full, will remain there
Let the settling dust cake the lipstick on it

I share my time with the whiff of your perfume
Its delicate memory visits with laughing ghosts
They announce your return like ballet dancers
Each beauty's gestures mock better than the last

The last music we were listening to stopped when you left
The notes torment me on my hills of nightmares
When you fade into the wall I bumped my head
Or when you call me from the sheets to join you
And the coldness of my pillows freeze your sweet murmurs

My last wish is for all somber colors
Or colors of holy terror or dread
Drums of the color of one thousand years war
Drums of the color of coming thunderstorms
Drums of the color of the oceans in anger
Guevera's passion boiling in a tornado
The colors of all the rare great spirits

63

Agaba Mgbedike Mammy Water Ijele

The colors in the eyes of one at a cliff edge
The color of the wailing night wind in the tundra
Colors of danger in flames or ice
Drums holding the pure colors of loneliness
Drums of the colors of sorrow in deep bass
Drums dirging at the tip of each brush stroke
It is finished ! It is finished !
Like thunderous saxophones from desolate ruins

That Absence

There is something festive
In knowing of those flowers of tenderness
We planted in our hearts
There is something festive
In the secret of those flowers
Singing with one voice
There is something festive ...

Mountains cannot dull its timbre
Not when space is its steed
With time a useless bridle

Secure in my heart
Your love has planted with deep roots
A bloom no demon song can wilt

Because I always feel your presence
The gentle petals tremble
When passion soldiers strike with force
The iron gates of your love
Those who would take beauty with storms
And wish rivers up mountains
Blind fools in the garden of love
Those who have missed armies at the foot of love
Because they know not the magic of flowers

I have strained my heart, my love
Against the stony prison of convention
My pains of love have died and resurrected
They have died and resurrected a thousand times

Today, I live like a brittle desert plant
My life is watered by the oases of our memories
And every dry branch breaks with thoughts of your pain

It is all my fault and yet not my fault
That our flowers bloom there in secret places
Singing in one voice and triumphant in the dark
But do not hide your agony of cold dreams in sweet laughter
Bring it like good wine to our warm places in the dark
My heart is an empty goblet waiting for its sacrament

Lost Compass

1

I lost you my compass
When I needed you most

Here in the dust storms
In lifes hurricanes

Time has globed the flame
Against my moths eyes

Seaman in a dream
Ringed with dune buggies

Like those malarial mirages
Hammering my granite gates

Your memory haunts always
They will not stay away

My own haunts are littoral
I am beach bound always

The waves murmur like you
In the hour of passion

Like you they go away
Leaving me like beach sand

With hopes for your return
And wetness in my heart

2

The hours are cold and grim
Without your hearts blanket

And those evening bell peals
Of all your sweet laughters

Your voice is always ringing
Like festival wine in my head

Lithe like a conjuration
You flare and melt away

Like a farmers precious crop
In a dream of famine and fire

Your passion was a cushion
Your constancy was a mace

You moved in quickly always
Between me and the anvil of foes

And between your last smile
And these bankrupt moments

The clouds are nimbus only
White lightning without rains...

Waiting

Lost keeper of the hearts sunny temple
The deep in a wand
Soul of my most secret shrine

This blue sky becomes the desert
As I sing for you
Lost oasis of my dream

The days wear robes of silences
Conspiracies
Creation is acolyte of your absence

Where are my jungle denizens
Palling choristers
Bearers of the banners of the rain wind

What ranges in combat against noontide
But thoughts of you
They prevail like rain in July

I linger now on a desolate terrain
Desert and distances
They mock me with your false effigies

Today is the day of fugitive dreams
Fan of memories
That is what shines from the stars

The roof of the sky feels my heartbeats
Farm of agonies
Endless flock of gamboling birds

What demon path led me to you
And this cold end
Desert destitute of your hearts pavilion

That magic trap of your sweet essence
I alone know
Reveler in the storm of your dreadful passion

Take these whispers in the language of flaming hearts
Font of mirages

Elusive game of the stubborn hunter

I hang my regrets like banners in the sky
Aware of loss
Beyond any gates of dreams and waiting

Green Leaf

Green leaf of eucalyptus
Crushed by the hard fingers of time

Whiff of fruit no one can pluck
The air is heavy with your wild wild scent
Too light for your powers
The wagon-loads of years

Ankh of memories
Lead me to the tombstone of our hearts
I the baby in your great hand

And when our memories gather
And when they rise
Like the waves of the waters of a new world
Let us float away on its great waves

Let us feel again the vocal silences
Speaking only to our bubbling hearts
Savage and holy like first man and woman
With the virgin juice of palm wine in the mouth
The glinting beach sand challenging our glow
Sharing with us a new sun and stars
And the secret fires from the moons gold pot
With testaments and promises heavy in the air
As we feel tugs from the arms of the wind
Muffling our laughter with its friendly wrappers

Green leaf of eucalyptus
Crushed on the hard fingers of time

Let me savor this daydream of fools
Wishing back the scent of dry leaf

While hot winds are combing crevices
For the strong medicine of your absence...

Breakers

We come always in the gaits of breakers
Thunder in our bold limbs
Thunder in our voices

For what we all carry in our bold names
Will go in dalliance in the arms of the wind
And beach sand will wear its glinting patience
Ready for ever for the burst of our roars

We will return to sea like flakes of sInto the white silence of shimmering
turquoise
Flashes of ether on ghostly horses

Perhaps only expiring thunders robed like us
Remember the desert lightning of our hot breaths
Like stifled dirges murmured by the wind

Iroko in the Wind

You wonder what gives the iroko strength
You wonder at its bole of power
You wonder at this rock of the bush
Standing always in the face of the wind

It will shed leaves when it desires
Or when other trees desire some shade
The iroko appeases the vagrant wind
The thunderstorm of the dead rain-maker
And the rain wind of the forlorn farmer
With ridges barren from desert and devil
Nothing threatens this jungle lord

It is the loyal soldier of the troubled chief
When traitors tryst in the dead of nights
When the heart of stalwarts tremble in doubt
It is the housetop above the jungle trees
Calling out for the lost womans heart
Calling to cure and end all bleeding

What do the branches wail for now
When iroko root is deep in the earth
What do the branches tremble for now

It is you my love who lets me stand
I die without the sweetness of the earth
Without anchor in the largeness of the hearth
I die without the sweetness of the earth
It is you my love who makes me stand
The spirit of the fibers of the iroko spirit

The Return

I have come back , my love
I am the unwanted resurrection
The miracle hated by those condemned
The one who would embrace death
For pride and the music of the good name

For this one moment
I will be the unwanted evening guest
One hour after the forced good night

I will spread my heart like cards
But not for the love of one more game
I come to let you know that your kind is not a virgin birth
I have seen them before
I read your last words well
You came after me like the heat of giant bellows
Touched by evil spirits after the blacksmith had closed shop
Your words of blame and scorn were unreal
They came from the jungle of feckless lovers
From the great wilderness of two-tongued devils
They know that their market is full
So they will not haggle with zephrs
Cyclones are at their thousand gates
And their horizon is black with tornadoes

I am not a cyclone
And I am not a tornado
My passion is like a little stream
It flows gently from the fountain of great hearts
It will never run dry
The threat of the desert gives it strength
And the harsh sun keeps its renewal promises

I know you are impatient with promises
You are the queen of festival dreamers
You cannot wait for tomorrow to be now
You cannot wait for the murmur of streams
Your heart you say cries for the thunder in things
For the thunder in things beware my love
The ancestors are not fools
The finger of death is in the sweetness of things

I came back to drop one seed of word
It is from the garden I once shared with you

When I met you I gave you a loaded gun
I am sad that you fired that gun
That loaded gun was my feelings
Blessed by something from the heart of deep waters
It had a gleam from the gun-shop of experience

My failure is for ever if I failed to let you know
My heart my love wears a bullet proof vest
Armor of finest steel against deceit

Beach Sand in the Evening

My heart is all beach sand
With all the bathers gone

Sunset leaves gold on waves
And ripples without meaning

How the beach changes face
With all the bathers gone

The footprints mock and jeer
Loudest without a sound

Like my heart benighted
With no memories of you

That, my love ,is my life
Beach sand in the evening...

Face in the Metro

1

That face of a woman
I saw in the metro

Dressed by a rainbow

The smile on the face
Of that strange woman

Dressed by a rainbow

2

Like the burst of a whale
From the deep blue see

I remember her

In a shower of pleasure
In a glow of peace

I remember her

3

Like something sharp
And something poignant

I remember her

That rain in the oasis
That meteor at mid-night

I remember her

4

Framed in my heart
Dressed by a rainbow

I remember her

The smile on that face
I saw in the metro

I remember her

5

That woman in the metro
The smile on that face

That face in the metro
Dressed by a rainbow

I weep always that
I cannot see her again...

I weep always that
I cannot see her again...

A Reflection

1

I know from one long afternoon
That slithers go with emerald eyes

A long afternoon of silent forests
Afternoons barren of denizen choirs

That one cannot read a source of tears
With no base salt to guide the script

That the elephant heart cannot prevail
Over the potency of the coded kiss

That the snake will always ride secure
On wheels of beauty and deep poison

With emerald eyes in the shadows
No one can read noontide mysteries

With a sky of pulsing aquamarine
With emerald eyes in the shadows

With emerald eyes in the shadows

2

What I heard was not what I saw
In the spread eagle glee of that heart

From its secret windows of mirth
Sweet voices from an ark of gold

From the dark waters of emerald eyes
Great sounds of silver cymbals came

And dance steps too from ceremonies
Billowing in sprays of stars and fires

With death in the waters of the emerald eyes
Behind shadows that will yield no secrets

In the shallow graves of the emerald eyes
Inside shadows that will yield no secrets

And I was a wanderer in her shores
And I was soporific in her power

In the shallow graves of the emerald eyes

3

And she spoke in a voice of secret hinges
And of festival and funereal sounds

Under blind stars of old memories
And from welts and lashes of pain

But what would I know of long taproots
Under stumps of the bitter leaf tree

Drawing from a well of frothing sadness
From the shimmers of emerald eyes

And with no witnesses there on shore
To rush to my drowning wails

Mirth shut its windows without sound
For the doors of police sirens

When spiders weave their webs for meals
Who hears their silent drums of death

Who reads the cyphers of their games
Except their lone prisoners of death

In their deep nights of evil spirits
What shepherds hear the black goat bleat

Who hears the silent drums of death...

4

This resplendent queen this petrifying beauty
You wove a prison with a web of laughter

Maker of miracles with mere heart beats

I surrendered to your sweet kiss of death

I surrendered to your goddess power
And to the winds of your emerald eyes

Old sails too weak for your demon winds
I surrendered my heart to your storm of fire

I will remember your grand supplication
I will remember your prayers for help

My knees of sympathy sinking like cloth
Into the fake hot tears of your imagined pain

I remember the strange beauty of your eyes
The shining shards of a shattered sorrow

Pieces from your windows of your heart of glass
The snare from your spiders table of fools

I will remember the white laces of your love
On the flagpole of your tales of woes

I will remember you and the slither of things
Alien creatures from your emerald eyes

I will remember all the bitter leaf tangs
On the tongues of innocents locked away

Behind the barbs of high prison walls
In the white afternoon or the deepest night

With emerald eyes in the shadows
The royal graves of the triumphant laws

With emerald eyes in the shadows
With emerald eyes in the shadows...

She Stands Before Me

She comes back like a calabash
From the bottom of the sea
And stands before me always
And will not go away
Because I brought the tinders
Which brought the termites home
My heart surrenders a silence
Like moonlight through the trees

And then she tells me all
And I cannot run away
She says I crushed the palace
But the queen has not been killed
And her voice is like a sting
And sounds like silver hand-cuffs
And because I know what happened
I cannot run away

She is the great drip drop
From a rain that needs no witness
After the tracks of shining tears
Blazing down her cheeks
Her witnesses are clear
And I cannot run away

Our sad yesterdays are restive
And they rise slowly from their tombs
Like the words of a dead poet
Whose thoughts have aged like wine
Like the sight lines of a marksman
They find my hearts bulls eye
I cringe from the truths of her cries
Like a baby's cry of need
Too deep for the shallows of my means

So her fingers follow me
And I cannot run away
And the shame of my naked heart
Shakes me without defense
And I cannot run away
She stands before me always
And I always turn into stone
When she comes back like a calabash
From the bottom of the sea...

Flower of Morning (for Elo)

Always the night mask comes to us
Always bold with a blade of blood
And always there in the sweetness of things
There when we are snug in the arms of dreams
Under the shade of the moon man's tree
There the night mask will always come
With a train of spirits singing in cyphers
No human tongue can ever read

And then all things will snap and fall
For this time of din and wails in the world
The Iroko's boulder heart will break and bleed
With graceful palm trees stories of surprise
In scripts of scars of twisted agonies
In fronds broken and fronds disheveled
Like hairs unkempt in the battles of the mad
With unseen enemies six-fingered in power
Where fern and tendril quiver in fear
Like hearts of antelopes in the lions spoor

When the singers cry for a song of carnage
No offerings of the living will appease them all
The masks of night and the spirits of the dark
No offerings of the living will appease them all

It is the hour of the kingly visitation
And no angel offals will be good enough
Oblations in their eyes are dust in the dark
No offerings of the living will appease them all
Because this is their time of carnage

But always too the morning returns
Always she stands like a flower in the sun
Flower of flowers crowned with sunrays
No revel of spirits will ever move her
She must stand there in the eye of the sun
In the calm shelter of tender leaves
A model of power beyond the night wind
Her anchor is a no name stem of steel
From the deep forge in the heart of things

The flower of flowers knows the one thing

She knows the night mask has no ears
For the din or wail that cannot bite
Her beauty glows like treasure from the deep
From lost fragrances from secret places
Ringed in incense ringed in silence
She lets the petals show their sheen
She knows always that nothing will matter
To the flower of flowers flower of morning
Windward now or against the wind
The night mask and the spirits cannot reach her
With head held high in the morning sun...

OF HISTORY...

The Spirits of Volubilis

I heard them there laughing and romping
The great spirits of the hills of Volubilis
I heard them laughing and romping there

They were laughing at two thousand years
Two thousand years of mouthful mirth
With two thousand years of eyes of power
Two thousand years of words and voices
Two thousand years of so many things
Those little ghosts on the hills of Volubilis

Their eyes were bigger than yesterday and today
They drew from the deep wells of pain and fear
From the darkness where clowns went for light
From the pit of our phoenix fears and passions
From the mountain of mirages and lambent flames
Where marble ghosts burn blazons in the wind

We will tire before their humor runs dry
We will tire before they end their peeking cries
We will tire before they pull back the great veils
The veils of natures calmest festivals
The sun will never tire of lighting that show
Because there is no applause here to make one pause

In the quiet of those rolling hills and plains
Land of the grandeur of a history still
That great beauty is there in the haze
Whatever commanded the Roman generals
To pitch in that wilderness of silent gods
Stone testaments of our naked hearts and heads
Our deathless rave to gore other bowels
For gold, for blood , one fragment o the winds back

Time did not quite cover a cistern there
Memorial for water below rusted iron
Memorial for wells memorial for other passions
A giant phallus lies there on a slab of rock
Memorial for power memorial for lust

There are inscriptions here on imperial arches
One more page on our meaningless noises

Only the wind reads this Latin for its use
The emperors inscriptions belong to ghosts
The laughing eyes of ghosts and tourists

We write we read we wander on
What new monuments will fill our wide eyes
Where in the vista of our raking hearts
Shall we till and water with hot sweat and blood
Deathless trees of such mortal winds

Chariots of mighty men once upon another hour
Clattered over these silent stones
Their lovers passions burnt this same air
With towers of flames reaching for the sky
Festoons of laughter ring their frames

The horizons swallow us with their wiped lips
And time closes the page for the next act...

& WAR...

Rodin in Biafra

As the unit quartermaster, I was called up one evening for the burial of a
Biafran officer friend who had dined with me in the morning of that day before
returning to the front for combat. I remember his name as Lt. Ihekenna from
around Umuahia. In this Biafran war note and poem, I try to recall and
therefore exorcise from my tortured Biafran mind, the painful memory of a little
boy, probably no more than five years old, who sat quietly and somberly on a
pavement watching us bury this dead Biafran army officer at Abayi-Ohanze, off
Aba, in the Azumini sector of the war...It was, I think, in late 1968... The grave
was shallow and unmarked...The posture of this gaunt and ghostly little boy
devastated by kwashiorkor, the dreaded
*malnutrition disease, was exactly the posture of Rodin's **The Thinker**...*

Something was old in those knuckles on a cheek
That pensive head with an unseen burden
Something that echoed something unknown
Something in that lull in the whistles of death
And Rodin sat at the public square thinking

The pose was perfect with elbow on knee
One forgotten arm rested on one reedy lap
But there was no artist there to see Rodin well
The artists were lost or dying in war
And Rodin sat at the public square thinking

All art was now expressed in blood
And when the taps of blood appeared to pause
Because all the enemies were having a break
And the whole planet seemed to hold its breath
And Rodin sat at the public square thinking

We placed a cold corpse on a lonely pavement
The residents of the house were dead and gone
Rats and lizards conferred with their ghosts
Perhaps only Rodin knew what they were saying
And Rodin sat at the public square thinking

In silent haste we buried the cold corpse
No bunting of tears could mark his passing
Passing was common like the setting sun
But we gave him speeches of valor and honor
And Rodin sat at the public square thinking

A jet swooped low with a rain of bullets
And man and woman rushed to shelter their heads
Like chickens fleeing from an army of hawks
A chill of death serrated their wails of fear
And Rodin sat at the public square thinking

Sirens warned of more hawks coming
The graveyard mounted a banner of gloom
With memories of the dead stirring in the wind
And each second was heavy with a frozen fever
And Rodin sat at the public square thinking

His eyes glowed strangely from inside his head
And his cheeks made him a thousand years old
What camp of pain is this web of bones
This five year old this shrunken Rodin
And he sat there at the public square thinking

No one knew where his parents were
When he ate last or whether he had friends
Which deserted homestead last saw his tears
And who heard last his sweet baby laughter

And Rodin sat at the public square thinking...

TALES OF THEIR PASSING
&
POEMS FOR THE GENERAL...

Tales of their Passing

The wind wields a mighty comb
And nothing hides in the underbrush
The wind wields a mighty comb

Fallen leaves will rise and walk
Wrappers reveal their pregnancies

All vessels will loose their hallowed lids
Over blessings or their secret horrors

That was how we read our stories
Sealed under the roof of our tongues

Hammered down by the Generals rules
With bolts of blood and fired screws

Who can forget the tales of their passing
The fire wood bundles of all our agonies

In mountain ranges at the public squares
Waiting for the flare to raze all woes
In mountain ranges at the public squares...

A Song For the General's File

Time will come again
Riding the magic broom of the wind
Time will come again

It will sweep the kitchen of memory
The agony of the chicken on the meat board
The sound of bones neatly broken
The gurgle of blood into cavernous drains

Of what use is the beauty of feathers
After all the smooth trowels of death

The cleaver hangs neatly on the wall
Its silence has joined the song of the great river
The great river sings in its silent flow

Of songs for all our bastard memories
Risen like saints from derelict graves

Of wisdom in the silence of the cut up chicken
In the roaring laughter of the pot on the fire

The cleaver hangs neatly on the wall
Its memory of blood is distant like planets

The cleaver hangs on the wall neatly
Time always keeps its treasures sealed
And the cleaver has faith in the hand of the wind

The Harmattan

O Harmattan
You hide your soldiers in the haze

You come with all the great medicines
In the tales of our ancient warriors

When they marched driven by chants of blood
We did not hear them
When they unsheathed their blades from their scabbards
We did not hear them
When they struck hard and beheaded their victims
We did not hear them
When they bellowed their songs of victory
We did not hear them
And when they marched into the breath of the wind
We did not hear them

We heard them in the tortured silences
Of the shattered homesteads
We heard them in the stifled dark sobs
Of the helpless widows
We heard them in the wringing grey wails
Of the baffled orphans
We heard them in the bitter leaf grunts
Of the lonely aged
We heard them in the thunderstorm pall
Over the soul of the clan

Wild horses of agony stormed after their trails of blood
Like crazed hens after the swoop of hawks
Tormented souls howled after them in cyclonic ghouls
And the village squares hummed the dirges of their coming

O Harmattan
You hide your soldiers in the haze

But how will you hide our bleeding lips
And how will you hide our broken skins
And how will you hide the sand in our teeth
And how will you hide the dust in our hair
And how will you hide the tears from our eyes
And how will you hide all the secret graves

And all those blows at the human spirit

The General hides his moves in the haze
What blankets can cover those trails of blood
What length of speeches and lamentations
What after-thoughts what wools of penitence
Will shield the General from disembodied eyes
The searing red brands in all his nightmares

The General moves faster than our ancient warriors
Swifter too than Harmattans and their haze
Of what use is speed to the enemies inside
Where nothing is faster than the human spirit...

A Song for their Second Coming

In your second coming
Remember always the festival of our birth

Even those who named us
Named us well
We were named after the Great River

They named us after our capacious hearts
They named us for our uncountable blessings
They named us after the promise in our skies
They named us after the abundance of our forests
They named us after our everlasting summers
They named us after the wealth in our earth
They named us for our great open laughter
They named us for our songs and our dances

And after the naming
We rubbed the chalk of birth on our wrists
We held it up for the world in pride
We mounted our dreams on all our highways
We sang of our hopes on our forest paths

On brazen buntings and on silken semaphores
We etched our plans for the world to see
We will conquer all heaven and earth
We will conquer all suns and stars
We will conquer all mirages on our hills
We will conquer all the horizons in our dreams
And sweetness will rule the pith of all things
And our world trembled from one bell in our hearts
A clangor of new visions and bold ecstasies

O festival of birth and still-born mirth
What rival ceremonies our hearts conceived
A carnival of blood and textbook murders

A demon confetti rained on all our heads
The barracks commanded a rival pentecost
With chalices of blood and satchels of gold
Ecstasies when gold is dipped in blood
And the General loved our show of skeletons
For each conscience exploded when the air stirred
Yells of greed thundered above our famished wails

What long miles in a dreadful alley
What hot nightmare of sordid images
Of embers too red for the anger of bulls...

A Song for Mgbedike
(with oja flutes, ogene music, and heavy chorus)

Every one sings the song of the great mask

Onye ajo chi puo n'uzo
Maka muo anyi egbuo madu
Onye ogbuolu o na n'iyi*

Usurpation is the badge of the brave
The gunman must usurp everything
And the village squares must go to hell

The gunman must usurp everything
And the city squares must be ringed with hell
With blades of fire to solder accord

Every one sings the song of the great mask

Onye ajo chi puo n'uzo
Maka muo anyi egbuo madu
Onye ogbuolu o na n'iyi

The gunman has crushed the fingers of children
He has poisoned the teats of mothers
He names his reign a time of the brave

The gunman has usurped everything
He has usurped the power over nightmares
He began for our nation his sweet nightmare

Every one sings the song of the great mask

Onye ajo chi puo n'uzo
Maka muo anyi egbuo madu
Onye ogbuolu o na n'iyi

While we were not in bed we dreamed
And loved our hot ovens of deceit
And we hoped for the joy of our meal times

To suspend all our bitter tears and pain
But balls of foo foo turned to porcupines

97

And scorpions swam in our peppery soups

Every one sings the song of the great mask

Onye ajo chi puo n'uzo
Maka muo anyi egbuo madu
Onye ogbuolu o na n'iyi

Our children erect their own sweet havens
And each haven is a school for wild gunmen
They learned their lessons from our great General

But who else is there to teach and show
Our fathers fleeing beyond distant swamps
Our mothers dancing naked in daylight

Every one sings the song of the great mask

Onye ajo chi puo n'uzo
Maka muo anyi egbuo madu
Onye ogbuolu o na n'iyi

Here is our new young ladies brigade
Practicing kidnapping without a sound
Only a kiss accents a deadly hug

See young men who jeer at pregnant women
Assassins of babies assassins of the rich
They walk the streets like epic heroes

Every one sings the song of the great mask

Onye ajo chi puo n'uzo
Maka muo anyi egbuo madu
Onye ogbuolu o na n'iyi

Make way for the General and all his cohorts
All his mistresses and alien counsels
Who make leisure from our public fortune

The great chorus who rise to his wand of power
Like the tide at the beach in our season of rains
All who have mastered the great song of our time

Every one sings the song of the great mask

Onye ajo chi puo n'uzo
Maka muo anyi egbuo madu
Onye ogbuolu o na n'iyi

(last line and song repeated many times for effect)

Who has a bad chi clear out of the way
 Lest our masked spirit kill somebody
  Who gets killed will come to naught

OF SUCCESS...

A Chant Of Success (for the *man*)

Kings queens sages and spirits
All ancestors wielding maces of fire

Hearts of laughter and coronation wine
Your name is honey on all their lips

> *Ah ha ! Oga— !*
> *You no go die again*

Tales of your beauty gleam in deep ebony
They cut the world like lightning in the dark

They laugh at darkness like the morning sun
Scornful of the distant evening bells

> *Ah ha ! Oga— !*
> *You no go die again*

Soon the sunset shifts from russet to white
Trains and acolytes in a voice of thunder

Summon all drums for the last hurrah
The last note from guardians of the grave

> *Ah ha ! Oga — !*
> *You no go die again*

Your head is higher than cathedral ceilings
And when your gait strikes the floor of marble

The little people tremble with furniture of oak
And chandeliers pale from lights from your eyes

> *Ah ha ! Oga — !*
> *You no go die again*

Your train glides past like something from the deep
In showers of light from your high palace walls

A track is wider than my bed of wood
But can size of beds measure the depth of sleep

Ah ha ! Oga — !
    You no go die again

From the snore of an idiot in the market of life
Songs of spaces on the wheels of dreams

One bed at a time for the king or the beggar
So many things we cannot have at a time

    Ah ha ! Oga — !
    You no go die again

We must hide when we hear your great voice
We dread your wisdom like potent lashes

Like red irons on ankles of some lost slaves
The laughter of sadists from an ocean of wine

    Ah ha ! Oga — !
    You no go die again

You frown at who will not notice your fame
Smoke of sulphur in a sultry afternoon

When the poor fear that sunset or dusk
Promises another day of pain and want

    Ah ha ! Oga — !
    You no go die again

If the amazon queen sings one song of hope
And misses a line from the honor you claim

Gods and spirits of the most distant worlds
Will feel the tremor of your passion and power

    Ah ha ! Oga — !
    You no go die again

Our wives must go to your next open tryst
When a new mistress forgets your purse of power

And no pissing angels notice your iron gaits
Or those wide arms all the little folks dread

Ah ha ! Oga — !
You no go die again

We are little mongrels and puppies from the bush
If your success thrives on our growls of hunger

The crumbs and bones from your table of fame
Will raise the volume of our cries of fear

Ah ha ! Oga — !
You no go die again

Secret ballasts drive us to the mountains of life
To give us views of jungle and wilderness

For the boats we need between the seven rivers
Where the spirits are drumming of bones and skulls

Ah ha ! Oga — !
You no go die again

When we sit on mountains and view the world
And think of those rhythms of bones and skulls

We could shorten our selves and lengthen our lives
For the notes and measures of those eternal drums

Unless Oga — !
You no go die again

LaVergne, TN USA
13 April 2010
179082LV00005B/57/A